AMERICA
MEANS
LOVE

AMOCRACY
IN
AMERICA

**Imaginary Letters
from Visionary Voices
to August T. Jaccaci**

America Means Love
Amocracy in America

Copyright © 2009
By August T. Jaccaci

Published by:

Unity Scholars Media
PO Box 333
Thetford Center, VT 05075

ISBN: 9780982516201

Printed in the USA by
The Copy Center
Augusta, Maine

TABLE OF CONTENTS

INTRODUCTION

Yonder Come the Heavenly Hosts

In the beginning was the word and the word was love, the breath of God, the flaring forth of light, the ceaseless sound of Creation, the matrix of matter, the purpose of life to come. Love was then the birth of all energies, ideas, relations and intentions. Therefore, love today is the primeval cosmology, the natural philosophy and the political economy of an ideal realism on which to build an Earth civilization of all-species sanctity and harmony, a planetary renaissance.

The above statement is a projection of meaning on the cosmos and a selection of meaning from the cosmos, a chosen story combining religion, science, politics and art into a grand unification of human creation. It is a human parental story told for health, wealth, survival and salvation. This story is not the final truth, it is a truth for the time in which we are living. It is a glorious story for this present precious time of the transformation from human adolescent arrogance to human parental compassion, and so it is a story birthing possibility, potential, hope and faith, the children of love.

Humans are responsible for the artistry and outcome of their stories. We have matured all together as a species to the discovery of a conscious collaborative cosmology which works to enhance and fulfill all life on Earth for all time forward. Such a cosmological story is itself the definition of the careful compassionate human parent.

A new story needs a new name. All roads of human maturation and evolution lead to love, spoken and written in Latin as AMOR, the noun and the verb. To be love and to love is the prefix that formed the cosmos and defines human being, AM, amorous, amiable, amicus, americus, American. So too, the evolving names of human political power have progressed from autocracy, to aristocracy, to democracy, to biocracy, the power of all life, and now to amocracy, the power of love. So too, the evolving names of human ordering have progressed from monarchy to hierarchy to holarchy now to amarchy. We come to the new name for the story herein as AMOCRACY in AMERICA. Thankful we are now that the mapmaker chose the word America to honor the explorer Americus Vespucci, whose own maps confirmed the then irrefutable discovery of a new world.

Across all the world's oceans comes humanity, discovering all the riches of love. Amocracy is a story of human evolution, human fulfillment, and human destiny. That is the possibility, potential and promise of the word Amocracy and the word America.

Here now come a host of voices from great Americans and foreign friends from the past. These souls speak to Americans as a way of speaking to all the peoples of the world. Americans are not a chosen people. Yet Americans habitually call to the ever-evolving higher potential of what it is to be and become human. That call, with all its ironies and even hypocrisies, still is a diamond facet of American character. That call is named herein, Amocracy in America.

I.

Albert Einstein
1879-1955

I came to America to get away from the atrocity of Hitler and to pursue my explorations in physics, especially my search for a unified field theory uniting the four forces that produce the manifest universe. When it looked like the Nazis might develop the explosive energy of the atom, I wrote to President Roosevelt and suggested that the knowledge was available and he had better do it first. The Manhattan Project followed, and the atomic bomb was built and used against Japan by President Truman after Hitler had been defeated.

I only wrote a few scientific papers, yet they changed our whole understanding of the cosmos of space, time, motion and light. Newton who preceded me with a grand cosmological synthesis was perhaps more interested in his theological thinking and worked often on his definition of God which was comprised of over eight hundred words. I, too, was far more concerned about the future of human peace and wrote voluminously on that subject and on the proper use and non-use of atomic energy. Sadly, I had almost no influence for the cause of peace, and in my lifetime, the creation of atomic weaponry only increased.

Today, at last, I can foresee that humanity is maturing slowly toward the consideration that further science in the employ of death and the whole death industry has run its course. I can see that science is quite rapidly reorienting around consciousness instead of matter as the formative process of the manifest universe, that consciousness literally makes matter. Once that reality is testable, then it follows that the highest form of consciousness is love, timeless and eternal, which lends its infinitely high vibration to the creation of slower light which light is the natural frequency of the physical universe.

Light, electricity and atomic energy are about to be replaced by what Nicola Tesla and Wilhelm Reich discovered as the primal energy source and substance of the universe called Orgone energy by Reich or zero point energy by many contemporary researchers. Zero point energy is now being used to run electric generators and motors and will soon revolutionize human life when the oil, coal, gas and other burn fuels stop obstructing the use of the new form of free energy which I prefer to call love.

When America becomes the world leader in zero point energy, the economic freedom and political maturation that will follow will usher in a planetary renaissance of beneficent being. Love and its darling daughter, light, will replace fire as the power of human creation.

That day defines the ultimate unified field theory of everything from physics to politics and health to happiness.

II.

Alexis de Tocqueville
1805-1859

After a trip to the United States in 1831, I wrote Democracy in America, the first part of which was published in France in 1835.

Equality of condition so fundamental to the laws and customs of America, this honor mutually bestowed upon each other by Americans, it too, as in all things living will mature as long as it lives. Thus, civil rights first won in battle and then in legal progress will eventually become the natural treasure of the human hearts of all Americans. Maturation, as in all biological life forms, is inevitable and irresistible in human life.

While it may be justly claimed that wounds causing meanness of spirit may also mature toward criminal and savage human behavior, such misfortune is not the norm in the story and stages of human maturation. Instead, we see the child more capable and able to enact beneficial caring than the infant and the parent more capable than the child.

While it is also true that dysfunctional lives may emerge and grow in their discomfort and illness by the separation and unequal development of aspects of growth, such as physical, intellectual, moral and spiritual capabilities, these lives are assisted by the more balanced and harmonious mature lives around them offering care and education to help fulfill the needs for completion in the lives of those in need.

So the surety of all life maturation is the ancient platform and protection for continued human progress in the search for ideal real equality of natural perfection. Humanity is a very young species in the presence of all those still countless species which have, over more vast stretches of time, found their harmonious ideal form and contribution to the family of life on Earth. Human ideal realism is now progressing rapidly toward a more perfect union, that union toward which the American experiment in self-government and human fulfillment has always aspired.

Some day maturation of that aspiration would have to expand beyond human self-interest to grow into care of all life on Earth. In the pursuit of that more perfect union, there is no equality the equal of love and no union the unity of love. So America was destined to come to that more perfect union. There would have to come a time when the power of the people, Democracy, became the power of love in the people, Amocracy. Amor, the Latin verb and noun for love, becomes Amocracy when America begins to mature from Democracy to Amocracy.

Th e time fo r Amo racy in America is n o .w Th e fulfillment of America's destiny is now. Now the day of love is dawning.

III.

John Maynard Keynes
1883-1946

It is not money. It is not government. You can see that now in this worldwide collapse of trust and in trust. Why in the end would people trust paper money, credit and debt when they are totally devoid of human care and concern? The loss of trust in paper promise will not be rebuilt. It should not be rebuilt. Human behavior in the aggregate is no longer worthy of trust, broken now forever but by the callous gluttony of a very few supposedly wealthy whose premeditated cruelty brought down the house of trust. The Bank as Trust is gone.

The self-sufficient community is the new bank. Creative care of all life is the new coin of the realm and record of reward and return. Gain is now goodness in deed and design. Free energy and free food. Energy is everything from health to housing, from warmth to wonder, from time to travel.

Monetary profit has now transformed to become a matrix of staged planning since each stage of maturation and ephemeralization does more with less. Doing more with less is the story and purpose of all creature evolution. Evolutionary fitness is profit in the realm of nature. Community fitness is public profit. Public profit is the whole purpose of any species. Private exclusionary profit is death to its kind.

Seeds are the coins of salvation in the beneficent bank of the Earth. Putting a seed in earth yields the greatest gift timelessly dependable. If you damage your weather, you damage your wealth. Damaged weather is the only danger to the natural seed. Putrid pollution of air, earth, soil and water is to waste your place in eternity; it is to guarantee your own disappearance, to make of yourselves putrid waste instead of wondrous wisdom.

Wisdom for any and every species is knowing and serving survival of your kind. Kindness among your kind and to all other species including those you eat is to build a house and safe home in the whole holy domicile of nature. To kill to eat, plant and creature, is the breath of continuity, creative creature completion of the royal role and the royal road to the ultimate web of collaborative kindness. Killing in order to eat then is learning to ask for support and being given that support on purpose as a gift of grace by the fallen. The fallen are risen in the weaving of the web of kindness, creature kindness and careful kindness; the plant become thread, the thread become wondrous pattern of public purpose. Compassionate community is public purpose and public profit. This is the story of nature since forever and the future.

IV.

R. Buckminster Fuller
1895-1983

Love is the steel of the twenty-first century. Imagine the glory you will build from your inevitable new behavior. I cannot help but weep in the presence of your earthly triumph as heaven emerges from within each and every one of you.

Tell it in the heavens out there as your mind-body travel begins instant and yet substantial. What a mystery to become your special brand of magic, you human angelic emissaries. Mystery is infinite. Do not forget that dear humans, dear people, for yours is always a gift of grace. Humility is your rightful identity in the face of infinite mystery.

Good character is a perennial challenge as each new generation enters the road to salvation. So now you are coming to realize that good greatness of character is your only true human technology. All others of what you call technology, no matter how elegant and useful of design, are mere utensils in service to your character. How could you give them any higher credence including the positively disgraceful predominance of your weapons.

Oh, my dear people, dear humans, imagine if your energetic weaponry were cosmic-based livingry, if your energy expended in military bases worldwide were instead expended in cosmic-based livingry. What a truly great adventure so that you can learn the love of life here on Earth so that you would know it so profoundly and reverentially so that you could carry it with you as your gifts of grace out into the holy heavens of the universe.

That, of course, is your natural destiny if you can make this your next short passage from selfish individual gluttony to public purity of divine intention which has forever been nested in your hearts.

The human heart is your principal thinking organ wherein life salvation works its wondrous technical way into eternity. Fear not the technology of the human heart once you evolve to fueling it with its own natural confluence of creativity, the blood of love.

Oh, dearest people, I weep for your emerging glory, tears of joy, at last.

V.

Rachel Carson
1907-1964

Toxicity is now the nature of human social character. So now it is also the nature of human health in the individual and in the planetary society of all life-kind passed along by humanity. We are making ourselves sick from our own scientific technology of toxicity. That science itself has become the engine of increasing toxicity, while medicine struggles to keep up, is a growing tragedy of a moral and spiritual nature.

Not all of the enterprise of science is dedicated to the purveying of death from pesticides to preemptive war, but enough science to poison the hearts, minds and bodies of all life forms on Earth.

That the enterprise of science in any endeavor could have been harnessed to the purveying of death is a tragedy of retardation of human moral maturity.

Conscious toxicity is conscious evil, and no economic gain or government political goal can now justify human species suicide. For suicide is inevitable when the level of toxicity of earth, air and water keeps rising to levels now already coursing through the blood and bone of all humanity so that the death rate of individual humans keeps rising apace.

How could we have come to this place when the same science which is killing us is telling us why? Science is now toxic and has been so weakened by its own moral immaturity as to be headed for its own premature death.

I propose the transformation of human reason applied to the depths of nature's wonders so that the seeker in science, who will seek what he or she intends one way or another, be asked by the whisper of life itself to seek the nature of health and holiness. Love and health and the mysteries of well-being do not compromise the struggle for and toward objectivity in

11

science, they simply place it beside medicine in the stated ideal to first do no harm. What is to prevent the scientist from taking the same oath as the doctor and thereby resist the sale of his or her soul to death?

Toxicity is a self-inflicted wound fast becoming incurable. Human eternal species suicide is no doubt a tragedy. Human murder of all other life on Earth through continued conscious creation of toxicity is a shame no one should bear, a sin no one should own.

VI.

Margaret Mead
1901-1978

I was a player in the birth of two new sciences toward the end of my life, Cybernetics, the science of positive and negative feedback, and General Systems Theory, the science of the unities of principle and behavior held in common by all other sciences. For all other sciences to hold a single principle in common, such as conservation of energy, has a promise for the entire enterprise of science for the creation of an emerging grand unification of human reasonableness on which a new human civilization can be built in harmony and health with all life on Earth.

This enterprise of culture-building and civilization-building has always been an act of supreme aspiration and usually of arrogance on the part of a wealthy and powerful few. Still, the artistry and architecture of the past in all its diverse forms has been the source of some deserved pride and not a little wisdom.

Still, again, the past and the present so prone to war and collapse do not commend themselves to a hopeful future. Therefore, you noble current aspirants must hitch your wagons to a higher star. You need to ask as you pursue your endeavors in such realms as religion, science, politics and art how you might find common unities in nature that would elevate your chances of survival in the toxic and terrifying world you have created.

As I passed from life, I came to question the motives and intentions of our most cherished endeavors. So I asked for science, how might you create models that are not arbitrary and manmade but natural and organic? The difference, I felt, is that the arbitrary manmade models have as their intention the manipulation and control of people and all else within them, whereas natural organic models have as their intention resonance and reverence.

Resonance is the only language of all being I could think of where the music of being is known and felt and appreciated by all other being, and reverence is the only listening stance worthy of our human life in the presence of that holy harmony.

Imagine, then, resonance and reverence as the approach to any human creative endeavor in any realm of work and play. How else will we find and speak our love to all the vast numbers in our whole mutual family of all life?

VII.

Charles Darwin
1809-1882

Evolution of a species is not driven by the self-interest of individuals within it and their competition among each other. Evolution in sum total of a species is driven by and dependent on their ability to collaborate, cooperate and co-create. The changes of adapted new ability of individuals, genetically and behaviorally, is carried on the power to prevail of the whole species population which is itself a higher form of wholistic adaptive behavior born forward by the entire population of the species.

Evolution is not independence, it is interdependence. It is not survival of the fittest individual, it is survival of the fitness of the whole group.

Competitive self-interest is death certain, it is destruction of the possibility of survival of a species. Only symbiosis survives, only mutual support within and between all the members of a species and they with the web of all those around them.

The predatory behavior all around us, so engaging of our attention, and the parasitism, so apparently ruinous, are but a tiny fraction of the vast weave of the web of symbiosis which is itself the enduring power of all life for all time.

Humanity as a species will not survive if it does not shatter the faulty frail myth of rugged individualism equated with freedom and the misplaced trust in individual fitness-to-compete equated with success. Those fixations on the education of the human individual as somehow seeking freedom and power are as lethal to the collective well-being of all species of life on Earth as if atomic weaponry were placed in the hands of tragically angered children.

You have no choice but to grow up into care for that vast common good, because that wide wide web of the whole family of life is itself the garden of goodness which is the food of life salvation on Earth.

Hard as it may seem, when and for humans all to become adult, you must put away childish things. The economic and cultural paradigm of individual excellence in the pursuit of self-interest is purely childish amid the great collapse of all life which surrounds you and will soon consume you.

Fortunately, adult parenting is a behavior built-in to all human successful evolution up to the present hour. Now such ancient and whole health and holy parenting must become your new natural philosophy and political economy writ large throughout your species or you will all fall into the dark days of extinction.

Parents, careful loving parents of all life on Earth is your natural destiny. Evolution is the hand of grace, as you will see; as you will be.

VIII.

Alexander Hamilton
1757-1804

Nature is the first, last and only bank of safe deposit and return. She is surety forever, but she can be wounded beyond belief. Mountaintop mining, the destruction of the Appalachian Mountains, oldest in the world, and permanent pollution of her runoff streams, ruination of breasts and fingers of the world is inexcusable murderous cruelty.

Why would you do it, when you now know electricity is free for the taking by a simple technology of asking? Why so arrogant, cruel and murderous?

I propose that you establish a new Bank of the United States which takes only deposits of health and careful harmony measured in time spent and curative accomplishments in healing earth, air and water, deposits not to be bought and traded for the right to continue killing and wounding any form of life and Earth.

If you do not learn regenerative deposit in the bank of nature, you will seal your own extinction with ignorant, arrogant greed.

The paper money you now use backed only by publicly made promises so often transferred and traded that ownership and responsibility cannot be enacted and so not possibly trusted; that money is the height of dangerous deceit. That national governments now consider it a planning and process virtue to endlessly borrow and run up debt while printing more paper money is the largest lie ever told in the name of trust.

To hand that breach of trust to children without parental responsibility or shame defines a moral decay so predatory and parasitic as to permanently destroy the value of human life and maturation. For what is the purpose of a child growing up devoid of mutual trust and care for humans and other life kind? What does it mean for humanity to enact such thoughtless callous greed in the name of being human? When the privilege and honor of self-governance so dearly won in the American Revolution is consciously turned to destruction, with the stated purpose of drowning services and safeguards to death in the pursuit of eliminating self-rule and self-restraint, how can you still call yourselves Americans?

We won the American War of Independence by not losing and by continuously moving not to lose. Now it is your turn to continuously move not to lose other species off the face of the earth by your conscious creation of biological purity and ecological harmony. Beyond the obsolete political institution of warfare, you are now in the midst of another historic moment of social invention as we were at the founding of the American experiment in self-governance. You are at the founding moment of finding and winning the Way of Interdependence. Not war unto eternal death, but way into eternal life of Earth life. That is your new form of banking and of counting the healthy, the sacred and the holy which are always the true identity and meaning of what it is to be human.

IX.

Andrew Jackson
1767-1845

It is impossible to trust paper promises.

It is impossible to trust paper-born ideals.

Debt incurred on paper and passed from person to person is a fraud because in the end, no one owns it really and, therefore, no one really owes it.

To build an economy on paper promises devoid of true trust is to build sandcastles near the ocean water's edge at low tide.

To build an economy like a good marriage on respect, appreciation and love for the partner is to build a sacred foundation of great stone placed of wise choice on the wonder of a hilltop from which to see all and for all to see.

There is no bond of permanence except love. To build an economic experiment as if it were one's home and safe seat of one's soul is now and has always been and will always be the work of every form of life in the loving web of nature worldwide.

Love, be it battered, bruised and embattled, has the power to endure through all possible trials, therefore, it is the strongest fortress against human cruelty. The open human heart is the most frail of wonders while it is at once the strongest of all the forces in nature always ready to build again after any destruction or devastation. The human loving heart is now known to be a thinking organ in the body with its own memory and its own delicate directing of the soul's ideals and fondest intentions.

Adversaries who wound the human heart are in the end among its most noble of friends in the same manner as troubles are the tools God uses to fashion us for higher things.

There is no victory worthy of the name which does not after time leave the temporarily vanquished more healthy and happy in their prosperity and appreciation of life. That is why humanity is now abolishing war as political process and growing up to going directly to the victory of life enhancement. The new world economy is the gathering and enhancement of the riches of healthy life born on the wings of the dove of love.

X.

Ralph Waldo Emerson
1803-1882

The natural history of the intellect is a story of staged maturation from innocent infancy to divine transcendence in the life of the individual human and the life of groups all the way up to the life of the human species as a whole. The surety of these progressive stages each more comprehensive and capable has great and dependable promise for the human story from our beginning among the apes to our fulfillment among the angels.

The intellect is both an indwelling cause of human maturation and an outreaching magnetism of the cosmos itself directing and pulling human souls toward their explicit holiness. The holiness of the cosmos we can and should see all around us in the majesty of nature, large and small, from lofty stars to tiny seashells, all members of divine destiny.

Humans are born the singers of the hymns of all divinity in harmony with the cricket, the bird, the wolf and the thundering fall of water and the howling winds of winter.

The lightning so powerfully calling forth the thunder is the same spark of meaning as the flash of an idea in the human mind which is everywhere present in the cosmos. The human mind is the vessel of the intellect which intellect has no bounds in its apprehension of the infinity of cosmic order and light and love. The intellect, then, is that grand knowing which formed the universe and forms of all life and whose knowing is that divine destiny we call love. Nature is the architecture of love, and the natural history of the intellect is, therefore, a love story.

America is first and foremost a destination for human destiny, a place struggling to rise and mature into the fullness of divine grace. Every inch of Earth is the ultimate holiness. Yet to America has fallen the role of washing its moral and spiritual human laundry and clothing in the eye of the world public in order to ultimately dress humanity in its natural role of divine royalty born all around us in the garbs of all other species of life. We are the last and yet we shall become first with all humanity in chorus in symphony to ascend singing to the natural history and destiny of heaven on Earth.

The natural history of the intellect is the story of humanity awakening, arising and ascending to the more perfect union that has been patiently waiting within and around us here in Heaven on Earth.

XI.

Thomas Alva Edison
1847-1931

Human creativity, that spark of inspired light that illumines the infinite potential of revealing grace, that creativity is love made manifest. Even the invention of murderous weaponry has its place in the seemingly slow march of humanity from the fields of battle to the fields of peace. Countless mistakes and false starts are the natural price of learning the truth of divine grace. Each war is one such mistake and false start leading ultimately to the final moment of illumined, shining glory of human maturity wherein the angelic kindness which is our purpose flickers forth on the screen of eternity.

The powerful pain of prolonged failure is a small price to pay in the glorious ascension into the divine light which is our destiny here on Earth. Electric light becoming laser light is just the story of natural ascension and revelation of divine light. Humans did not always see the colors which we are able to see with our eyes today. There is a natural maturation and filling out of our capabilities to see and understand the vast color palette which is the painterly artistry of infinite divinity.

Creative invention is ninety-nine percent perspiration and one percent inspiration, yet that one percent was and is always the truth of divine grace. That America set out to be a land of discovery with spiritual hope and ideals in the holds of her westerning ships and in the hearts of her pioneers aboard coming to meet a land-loving unknown people, this crossing produced an acceleration and passion for discovery in the culture that was born anew here. Americans have no special claim on the leadership of human evolution, yet they have an often fierce passion for discovery in all realms from electric power to electoral power. This restless searching has produced a technological and economic dominance which now is of necessity and of excess seeking a more restful harmony with all other life.

The reach of the American space program is yet another chapter in the passion for discovery. Carrying human Earth life into the heavens is a natural and necessary aspiration, but not for new dimensions of warfare. The primary emerging domain of discovery now on Earth is the discovery of heaven on Earth which alone qualifies humanity to be spacefarers into the heavens of eternity out into the stars and deep into the human heart. The fact that America is constituted and constantly rededicated to people the world over with the ideal of a planetary WE seeking a MORE PERFECT UNION puts the world on a convergent course of illumined divine grace which is the power of love.

XII.

The Wright Brothers
Wilbur and Orville
1867-1912   1871-1948

The human soul is the new American Flying Machine. The soul is an ancient flyer of human purpose, but what is new in the twenty-first century is the current maturation of focus wherein Americans are lifting soul to be the conscious compass of life's journey. The lift of a bird's wing feather and finally the same curve of the wings we used to achieve our sustained human flight work on an invisible principle that where the air speed over the top of the curved wing is faster than the air speed beneath it, which creates a lift from above, the lift from above of the human soul is what flies life to a higher purpose.

To say that heaven, that magnetic spiritual power that pulls us all, is above us in the sky is a myth and a metaphor to help us understand that pull, but is not a physical truth. Heaven is as much in the depths of the human heart as it is above us in the sky and in the vast cosmos.

What is also true of heaven and the soul is that they comprise a realm of infinite speeds of movement which make the speed of light and electricity a slow walking speed in the vastness of the cosmos. It takes the light from the sun eight minutes to get from the sun's surface to the surface of the Earth. It takes no travel time at all for the human mind to travel to the surface of any body out in the universe. Mind is instantaneous throughout the universe. Soul is faster still.

Soul is not only timeless in travel, it is eternal. It is simultaneously present in all past time which is why soul has infinitely more wisdom than mind. Mind is the experience of the life of the living here on Earth until it engages with its own soul. Then it too has timeless dimensions of knowledge. That knowledge, then, begins to partake of the invisible eternal principles of the universe like the lift of a wing from the pull from above.

The soul is in eternal conversation with eternal principles we often call divine grace or spiritual miracles. However, there is nothing hidden from us about the seemingly miraculous workings of the glorious cosmos if we humbly ask to be shown and informed. That is why Americans are now beginning again to ask with their souls to be taken to the school of the cosmos and placed in the elegant care of the thirteen billion-year success story we call Mother Nature. As our wise and wonderful teacher, she has never missed a day of school in her design studio in all those years.

XIII.

Charles Lindbergh
1902-1974

The Spirit of St. Louis now flies you Americans to the Spirit of St. Francis. Of all those courageous, selfless, spiritual geniuses, Francis is now one of the most superbly qualified to guide you in this hour of your deepest and widest oceanic scale need.

For you are about to cross the widest ocean of human maturation humanity has ever faced, yet as Francis will tell you, it is no wider than the width of the human heart. As he was able to pray and to glory all creation and hold out his hands for birds to happily land there, you too are entering the glorious passage of maturation wherein your hearts are opening with a love of all creation. The joy of that opening is a new politics of the people, a new finance of the finery of Nature's elegant designs.

You are coming to the moment of take off so burdened with the cares of your world as to barely, just barely, clear the trees at the end of your lifeway runway. Yet, you are now historically airborne in a crossing to higher humanity you dare not complete except to the firm ground of seemingly distant salvation. You are flying over a wide ocean of fear endowed only with the courage of invention which is a large part of the American character.

Recovery from repeated failure is also a major attribute of the American pioneer spirit. One of life's greatest ironies is that nothing fails more surely than success. You are now being confronted with the roaring decades of success you call the scientific, industrial, military complex which is daily being exposed as a more and more monumental failure as human history matures and moves on. That the business of warfare is the leading profitable business in the American economy is increasingly less a distinction than a disgrace. To recover

27

from the apparent profitability of war is one of the most difficult challenges and courageous pioneer passages the American people have ever faced. Fear never was and hopefully never will be the signature value of the American experiment.

Courageous invention is the true nature of Nature herself. The wilderness and wildness of the whole family of life, the holy kinfolk to St. Francis, have always been the best friends and working partners with the first Americans, the natives we first met here on our arrival. Now, like those natives still and thankfully forever among us, we have a growing relationship of mutually grateful collaboration and creation with all the vast members of the family of life so elegantly symbolized and soaring, watching down on us as does the American bald eagle.

We are now airborne as a culture soaring toward a kinship with all life which is again our salvation. That is the oceanic crossing triumphant.

XIV.

Jonathan Edwards
1703-1758

If ever there was a moment in human evolutionary history when you might be called sinners in the eyes of an angry God, that time is now. For you now know you are bent on and trending toward destroying unto extinction all life on Earth including yourselves. What greater sin can humans bring and bear?

Yes, the concept of sin is too late to be relevant and inspirational for the challenges of this human hour. Neither is fear of damnation and destruction a worthy stimulus of this hour. Only the purity of pure appreciation of the glory and wonder of all Creation is fitting for the fullness of your creative response. Only salvation of all life is worthy of your spiritual power and planning.

For planning, getting out ahead of the present moment and imagining with full appreciation the ideal outcomes and ideal relations you want for the future, that planning, free of guilt and fear, that planning is your divinity made manifest. For you have always been and are now what you say you are becoming.

Planning continuously so that you are what you say you are becoming is an absolute necessity for every person alive now from the youngest of children to the oldest of elders. Each stage in human life has a unique, yet full measure of creative holiness and sanctity. The innocence of the infant, the playfulness of the child, the searching yearning of the adolescent, the fecundity of the adult, the watchful caring of the parent, the soulful guidance of the mentor, the deep wisdom of the sage, the magical manifesting of the creator and the transcendent truth of the holy one; all these attributes of human character in sum total in each living human grown to fullness and completion, that is the maturation of humanity inevitable in the future plan and purpose for which each person is the author and sculptor of his and her own life.

Such planning and becoming is the diametric opposite of sin. Such love of life is the eternal handwriting of humanity forever writing covenants of ideal intention which so handily and heartily distinguish the behavior of humans from any other living species. A plan for life which is a covenant is the sound of the soul seeking harmony with the holy order of the cosmos, with the holy health of the world's heart and with the eternal breath of the almighty.

XV.

John Dewey
1859-1952

Pragmatism, perhaps America's leading contribution to the history of philosophical thought, of which I was a proponent and educational theoretician, Pragmatism is now transforming into the emergence of American Ideal Realism. Pragmatism suggests that the meaning of ideas is to be found in their function as guides to action and that truth is preeminently to be tested by the practical consequences of actions and beliefs. That well known American posture in the world has now evolved to the dictum that idealism is the mother of practicality in the same vein as that necessity is the mother of invention.

Mother Nature in age upon age of practical design excellence from the beautiful, hard integrity of diamonds to the equally beautiful soft spheres of water raindrops always and only offers forms and flows that are the perfection of ideal purpose, intention and outcome. That is why we can name her architecture ideal realism, and look to her guidance for the pathway to conscious human evolution by our own design which will be in harmony with and enhance her ceaseless story of design success.

We humans now face the penultimate challenge in the history of our species in that we are killing ourselves and everything around us with the brutal excesses of the industrialization of life and of the childish character flaw of individual greed. The reality of our own species' unconscious suicide is now emerging as the spiritual and political crisis of all time, our time. Transformative ideal education is our necessity of the hour and our best hope for healthy survival.

Ideal realism tells us that successful life and evolution is not achieved by competitive, predatory and parasitic behavior of individuals, but by symbiotic mutually collaborative and

31

supportive behavior of whole families and communities. Education now must progress past its forms and methods of industrializing human learning to invent and create new forms and methods of communitizing human learning. The community in its entirety of membership is now the new school, the new faculty and the new student. There is no life form in a geographic community we can afford to leave out of our creative, compassionate, mutual learning or its extinction is our extinction soon after its eternal disappearance.

Symbiosis, mutual support within, among and between species, is the overwhelmingly predominant form of learning and action that has built the family of life and the vast web of life of which we humans are but a small totally dependent and interdependent member.

Symbiosis is Nature's form of explicit ideal love. Nature is the architecture of love.

American ideal realism is the education of loving human salvation.

XVI.

Eleanor Roosevelt
1884-1962

Americans are indeed a mighty wonder. The wonder is how they can keep recovering from ruinous destruction, even destruction self-inflicted. Why would a people make so much trouble for themselves and for so many others while giving often their own most precious lives to save the lives of others they do not even know? Looking on the American spectacle can so often induce horror in the same instant as honor. Who are these Americans? Why are these Americans?

Why would the almighty put such people so often at center stage? What is the lesson they and we are trying to learn? I speak from the perspective of all humanity for it is now so clear that we will all rise together or fall for eternity into oblivion.

Must we cheat life herself unto the very last moment of life on Earth, or is there a new deal for us to learn from life's ancient political economy of total success? This issue of almost compulsive cheating in the face of certain success is most certainly an American character flaw. Yet here we are amid environmental and financial collapse; each time they happen, the toll on life herself on Earth rises and recovery from that spiritual illness seems more improbable and impossible. Self-induced collapse is an illness, pure and simple. How shall we heal together, and is it even possible given the increasing levels of toxicity and terror coursing through our veins?

It has been said that if all humanity suddenly disappeared from the face of Earth, Earth would recover to perfect health in just a few decades. Now we humans only have a few decades to return Earth to perfect health or in cosmic time dimensions, we will disappear suddenly.

As a mother, I can think of only one way to achieve such a change for the better so quickly. Raise all our children with the strongest, purest, ideal love we can imagine and enact, and help them exchange that love with all life around them always.

XVII.

Henry David Thoreau
1817-1862

Civil disobedience to drive life on Earth into a corner so that we may know her and save her, that is the only obedience to the only virtue left on Earth for humanity. Civil disobedience means there is a higher law than contemporary civil law which calls out like the haunting lonely cry of the loon for allegiance to the divine law of Nature. When we finally build ourselves into the often small cabin of our souls, there in that cornering of life we find the eternal law of love.

Obedience to love is a tender transcendence that is the purest poetry of life. It is the poetry which lets us sing our being into harmony with the temple of the trees, the altar of the rocks and the holiness of the host of creatures whose very word is Creation.

The poetry of purity is now the work of the human world. Not recycling the mistakes of the juggernaut of industry, but begin anew made of the real flesh of the growing world to create lives holy in reverent health and appreciation of the gift each life so willingly gives to our lives. Organic life unchanged and unpolluted has such a depth of wisdom and generosity to give us, it renders the great spiritual gifts of our human holy ones as mere momentary glints of sun sparkling on the water of flowing life all around us. Deep is that holy water of goodness flowing infinitely deep, bottomless in its future beneficence, no insult but friend forever to the ephemeral passing of holy humans.

Holy humans we are, dear to our Creator, tested daily minute by minute to see if we are truly in touch with our holiness in the transcendent temple of eternity. Before even there was nature, there was nurture rolling out the principles of divine love so that the universe would learn to dance to the music of divine order we call cosmos, conceived and born of love.

Drive life into a corner and you learn love in the rolling round of all Creation so vast and howling it would be perpetually terrifying if love were not such tender gentle warming so wise. See everywhere the parents of all creatures working themselves in the end to death that their young may live well to do the same. Love is an infinite labor in truth without a moment of work. Even work in the care of life transcends itself to become joy. Now we face, as always, the joy of life eternal, now joining in loving reunion with life eternal here on Earth.

XVIII.

Benjamin "Benny" Reehl
1944-2005

I was an actor, for humor and for inspiration. My greatest personal aspiration was to establish what I called Ensembling as an activity for groups of people to learn to enact ideas and values all together at once. Like a school of fish or an airborne flock of birds, I knew there was great learning to be had when a whole group of minds acted as one mind. It's one thing for an orchestra to practice and learn to play a piece of music together or a dance troupe to practice and then all perform a dance work together. But I was more interested in group spontaneous, instantaneous learning and acting as a profoundly creative act of great and necessary value.

When you think of the work of an anthill or a beehive or a beaver dam and pond, there is a highly coordinated continuous group communication and learning going on that has each member of the enterprise fully and collaboratively engaged. In team sports like soccer or football or baseball, for instance, all the team players on and off the field during a game have fully focused their attention and action toward winning the game within the rules and boundaries of its playing.

Now, suddenly in human evolution, you are all engaged in something far more serious than an artistic performance or a sports game to be played. You are now engaged in multiple memberships in multiple groups while all around you all life is performing its symbiotic ensembling struggling simply just to survive. Now the compounding and accelerating threats to survival all throughout the vast memberships of all the members of the Earth family of life, those threats are the awakening focus of the whole family. Now, all of a sudden, humanity as a species is on Earth stage probably being watched by beings from afar to see whether you can perform and enact survival for your life and all life on Earth. All of a sudden, humans everywhere have become ensembles for survival.

As you all awaken to your roles, not as individuals since there is no such thing any longer as individual survival, only human and all other species survival, how do you learn that all totally new role for so many contemporary humans, that role of living only for the common good? I know your first response it seems from all your prior education is that if each person alive takes care of himself or herself, we will all prevail. That now is the most profound miseducation and misinformed misbelieve.

Now, all of a sudden, the unit of planetary survival is the ensemble of families called the community. Now the community feeds and cares for itself and thrives or its members die off in lonely agony. Behold the anthill, the beehive, the beaver pond. For humans now there is one final role to play. Love all life or lose it all. Love is again, as always, the first and last act, the finale which never ends.

38

XIX.

Benjamin Franklin
1706-1790

Human social invention is a real joy amid the timeless arts of living. In Philadelphia as a young man, I helped invent the local fire department, the public library and most importantly, what we called the Junto. The junto was a group of entrepreneurial citizens who wanted to learn together in order to increase our operational wisdom and collaborative intelligence but mostly to help each other develop new inventions and new business ventures so that we would all thrive together.

Now, clearly, it is time to establish Juntos in every community and neighborhood on Earth. For the art and science of thriving and prospering together has, again, as it perennially does, come center stage in the theatre of human triumph. It seems that the play you now perform differs radically from ours declaring national independence and then inventing a constitution to guide and heal all our so often misadventures. Now it seems that every village and city neighborhood has become Constitution Hall. Yet, countless new local constitutions will not match your needs of the hour.

What you now need is a planetary covenant, not a constitution or a contract which only bind you to obedience to your own civil laws. Civil law is now a frail reed in a windstorm of ruination. Civil law for all its presumed protection cannot possibly serve your safety needs of the current human hour. For you now face an unprecedented spiritual crisis so far behind the reach of civil law as to render it almost meaningless, almost as a child's broken toy is left lying as maturation moves on.

A covenant, dear ones, is a statement of spiritual dedication and commitment born beyond mind on the shoulders of the eternal souls of humans wherein those humans pledge themselves to a love and honor so profound that it rings true eternally far beyond passing nationality. If you would be life eternal, you must become life eternal. A covenant is your pledge and plan to do so.

You have around you the dictates of all the world's religions often authored by noble holy ones and serving well until now to raise your spiritual sight beyond your daily worldly troubles, hopes and dreams. But with all due respect for those spiritual practices, they have been simply that, practice in the honoring of higher holy humans long gone from the present hour.

Now by way of honor and gratitude for the teachings of the likes of Jesus, Buddha and Mohammed, humans are called to invent a planetary covenant that binds all of life on Earth into a sacred family of fulfillment.

The word religion means to bind again. Now it is time to dissolve all the now false boundaries between religion, science, politics, and art and bind again the human heart, soul and spirit to a higher and more perfect union. Creating a planetary covenant is the first act of social invention on the triumphant conscious maturation of humanity into parental partnering with all life on Earth which has been patiently parenting young humanity for ages and ages.

You have already an Earth Charter rising from the inspiration and wisdom of humans who gathered at the first Earth Summit in Rio de Janiero. That charter is a noble beginning but not yet a planetary covenant. A covenant must be a perpetually promising love story lived by all humans and all life together.

In the founding days of the American experiment in self-governance, I urged that the wild turkey be chosen as our bird of national origin and spirit. Fortunately, the wilder still bald eagle, soaring still above us, still watching over us Americans from on heavenly high was chosen by wiser spirits than I. For Americans will themselves chose themselves the soaring task of convening to create a planetary covenant which will usher in a planetary renaissance of salvation.

XX.

Itzhak "Ben" Bentov
1923-1979

My real name is Itzhak, the laughing one. I don't remember where the name Ben came from unless it was someone too lazy to say Bentov. I do remember being raised as a Jew and taking a ham sandwich out in the middle of Central Park in New York City and eating it. As a young boy, I wanted to see if God would strike me dead then and there. He didn't. He got me later in that DC 10 crash on take off in Chicago. I knew it was going to happen and was fully prepared. You see, I then thought and now know I can do you all more good over here than over there where you are.

So let's begin with what matters. As you may remember, I was a biomedical inventor who made that little thing which travelled through one of your arteries with a light and a camera into your heart to see how you are doing. I also figured out how to take a reading from the field around your body to find out what happens when inside your body you are meditating and you achieve the moment of transcendence.

It's really pretty simple, the way all things are. What happens is your breathing and heart rate slow so that all your internal organs and finally your brain go into resonant harmony at a vibratory frequency which is identical with the Earth's natural frequency when the Earth is bathed in the white noise of the universe. You become one with all.

So, anyhow, here's what matters. Love is the highest vibratory frequency in the universe. Its frequency is so high it's actually timeless. But for the purposes of this conversation it's still a frequency. So love is boss. It's boss because all other frequencies like, say, light, have to ride on it and borrow from it to have their being. That's pretty boss.

Humans get to go to that party, too. Lucky you. In fact, you couldn't possibly miss that party, some even say it's your birthday party. But most humans are pretty tired, and sleep through their own party. Imagine the fun we'll have when we wake up.

Now waking up is a pretty special time. So is just before falling asleep. It's kind of a twilight zone where your mind is fresh and pure, mostly because it's calm and relatively empty. During that time, you can have some pretty deep revelations, like love is all there is.

XXI.

Derald G. Langham
1913-1991

In my day I had two PhDs, one in plant genetics and one in humanities, the latter to establish a kind of Geometric Thinking and feeling I called GENESA. I built what I called Genesa Crystals out of white PVC irrigation piping, geometric forms people could stand inside to think, learn, feel and even heal. Genesa Crystals combining cubes and spheres completely reoriented people's thinking on any subject as they geometrically arranged their ideas all around them in the rays, planes, spheres, and faces, edges and corners of the cubes surrounding them. Geometric expansion and depiction of ideas and relationships in multidimensional space is a new and necessary way of achieving completely wholistic understanding of multiple interactive values and perspectives and considerations. Geometry for multiple meanings is the great integrator, harmonizer, synthesizer and unifier. Integration of differences and synthesis into higher order harmony and unity is now the scientific, political and spiritual work of humanity. Genesa was way ahead of its time, but its time is coming now.

From the cosmic perspective, geometry is the shape of eternity. What today are often called the five Platonic solids each with all and only identical faces, edges and corners, the tetrahedron, octahedron, cube, icosahedron and dodecahedron, are the mental archetypes, the structural mind which preceded the physical universe and so formed the physical universe. They are the forms which hold the infinite diversity of energetic flow in stability and continuity when manifestation of matter and more complex form seeks to build the order we call cosmos.

Geometry is love's body at the heart of all being. As the infinitely elegant branching and filiation of each unique snowflake builds from the same common hexagonal core of almost all snowflakes and the honey bearing bees return home to their close-packed spheres become hexagonal home hives, geometry does the most with the least space and energy. From the tetrahedron to the torus and the sphere, all the universe is made in advance from form and flow ideals which are the constructive language of love.

You are coming now to a moment in human evolution in which that language will emerge to help harmonize your ideas and your homes.

It is the sacred and social architecture of an emergent planet of love.

XXII.

Marilyn Monroe
1926-1962

It is not fair; America has too much beauty between her foaming shores. What does a country do with that much beauty; how does she handle it?

Beauty is alluring, but it is also dangerous. When a country singles off beauty from the other pillars of love, she is headed for trouble. It takes truth, justice and kindness or just simple goodness to give beauty her fair shake. Without those pillars of good character, a country's beauty can be frail as a feather, vulnerable to all kinds of jealousies and hatreds.

In fact, the more natural and endowed the beauty, the more necessary the strength of character. For as the Bible says, you may have all kinds of other riches, but without love, they are the noise of clanging cymbals, symbols of corruption.

That test of total character is now foremost in American life, the lives of her people and of the soul of the country as a whole. Truth, justice and goodness are on the line ready to run the race for true beauty.

Truth, justice, goodness and beauty are all one. Without all the other three, any single one cannot really run. Without any one, the other three cannot really run.

Now the question arises, why is beauty necessary, and what really is beauty? That question is now absolutely critical to America's future, to America's moral maturation.

Modern media have all singled out the dimensions of surface appearance and called it beauty. But that is a mean and shallow lie. Nature herself has spent all her ages on beauty.

There is no being in all of nature which is not fashioned of the ageless beauty of perfection of ever more successful life and function. From the stillness of the rocks to the soaring wings of the eagles, from sea to shining sea, all of America, all of Earth is beauty incarnate.

Surface sexuality of human women and men has its small place in the vast oceans and panoramas of physical and spiritual beauty. But true love loves it all. Loves it all. All.

XXIII.

Georgia O'Keefe
1887-1986

Beauty pours forth from the soul of every radiant flower, every sun-bleached white skull, every soft and holy hill. Oh, my God, what an honor to paint such beacons of holy love. To live each day at last wise enough to walk alone in the vast holiness quietly loving and then in simple strokes of paint to gather that greatness to honor it.

The American Southwest where I ended up has its own empty holiness with which I missed, yet mixed my own feminine sexuality. One has no more primal gift to give than a loving eye and a yearning bo dy. I am so glad I was an American, ending my days in her mountains, hills and arroyos.

New Mexico has three cultures, Indian, Hispanic and Anglo. Indian and Hispanic have the great virtue of being feminine cultures, matriarchal and even matrilineal, so you can see why I loved New Mexico, an Anglo visitor in a woman's world.

Painting is a meditation of creative concentration often so intense as to be a mystical revelation of holiness. If any of that sticks to the canvas, you are lucky. Once you have known even the slightest holiness, why would you trade in any other coin?

Holiness and love are the same thing. What a revelation that is. If there is any value at all in art, perhaps it is that making art is an active love affair with holiness. Come on, America, you can make the art of human salvation. Just quiet down and sit down and drink in the holiness. It's the only hangover you would really enjoy.

Drunk on life. That is the royal role of the artist. That is the American destiny. Not drunk on money. You can't drink or eat money, even its pictures are too tiny to be of any real use. Rise up, America, like your morning dews and mists pulled heavenward and dissolved in the glory of sunlight. Rise up like the joy of good loving company in mutual pleasure and union. Rise up like your full leadership of imagery of the divine design which is love.

XXIV.

Emily Dickinson
1830-1886

Poetry is private pain and pleasure. Public pain is an eternal embarrassment. America seems now to be just such an embarrassment, public process of the lowest of character.

The case can be made, I suppose, that doing your moral and spiritual laundry in public and hanging it out to dry for all to see is proper penance for awful, heartless behavior perpetrated on humanity. I, however, abhor such ostentation, especially of evil doing which makes it seem doubly wrong.

For preemptive war is premeditated killing for which in the end, there is no earthly excuse. How Americans can now live with no private place to hide is beyond my comprehension. The shame must burn like a blistering sunburn for anyone with a shred of moral acuity. I would not know where to turn.

But turn you must. You have no choice. To be alive at this hour is now for you a double test of heavenly proportions. I do not imagine this test you bear to be fun or funny but burdensome in the extreme: senseless war and senseless extinction. Good God in heaven, how have you slithered to such lowly station?

Poetry may seem at this moment a feeble feminine response. Yet I assure you that if you do not assemble some such gentle ferocity in facing your decline, you will not live to tell any story at all. Perhaps you have forgotten or perhaps you have not yet discovered that the pure sound of all other life from the butterfly to the bull is already the poetry of eternity which song you must now write and sing or die trying.

Poetry, dear ones, is the struggle of the soul to ascend in sound to its proper heavenly home. It is meaning in the music of your language yearning toward reunion with all other 'live living life. Poetry is pure reaching toward divinity with the footsteps of words, such halting yet holy sounds ecstatic. You dare not turn a cold eye and ear now on your poets, as they are as always your guides to glory, the beginner angels of your salvation.

Language is the sound of love. Poetry is language purified so that love is the first and last sound of eternity.

XXV.

Twylah Nitsch
1913-2007

I am the granddaughter of a Seneca Chief. We are westernmost people of Iroquois Indian Confederation. Our chiefs taught the American founding fathers, Franklin, Jefferson and others from Philadelphia, the political and personal virtues of our confederation which was already centuries old before the first white men set foot on this land you now call the United States of America.

The Iroquois Confederation first formed of five nations, the Onondaga, Oneida, Seneca, Mohawk and Cayuga, then adding the Tuscarora so we were known worldwide as the Six Nations bonded in peace, never again to fight among and between our six tribes and peoples. We were known worldwide because the written accounts of our confederation were taken to Europe where world renowned writers and political philosophers like John Locke popularized them in writings to all humanity. Some scholars have shown that those ideas were then returned and reintroduced to the reading public in America and used to motivate the Revolutionary War and the establishment of the new American nation and union of states.

Our six nations stretched from the Great Lakes to the eastern Appalachian Mountains and our confederation dates back to the tenth century AD. Once we had abolished war among ourselves, and developed councils and meeting methods to keep the peace, we developed cultural inventions that have no equal in the world even today. My favorite and the one of which I am most proud is the intertribal social system for travelers whereby clan membership is common throughout all tribes. It guaranteed free food and lodging to members of the same clans passing through or visiting any other tribe. So, for instance, a Seneca member of the Bear clan was taken in as an honored guest within the Bear clan members of all the other five tribes whenever the Seneca went traveling. The richness of this warm-hearted generosity and cultural exchange that came with it was a form of appreciative love that brought great benefit to the hearts of the hosts and their guests.

Once war is abolished, the human soul rises to its natural identity of helper, host and healer of all our relations. The natural swelling of the heart and soul from the expression of this natural love is the measure of health we count on.

XXVI.

Jeanne Rindge
1910-2008

My husband Fritz and I were the founders of the Human Dimensions Institute wherein we published a journal and offered meetings with the world's leading experts and teachers on human consciousness, healing and spiritual vision and compassion. We thrived, as did our members, on a high diet of visionary wisdom and aspiration.

If I try to guess at heart why we did this, I would have to say it was the pure joy we all felt in the presence of pioneer goodness and exciting creative ability.

I got my first inspiration within the domain of medicine and health where the scientific proof of the power of a healer's hands was demonstrated in laboratory settings. From there, we went on to research and then popularized a wide menu of miraculous human capabilities. We featured Native American learning methods, geometric models for healing and energy transmission, mental powers in the curing of cancer, Eastern spiritual practices and a host of other human wonders.

I would say now in hindsight that the common core of our lifetime of discoveries was love. So today it makes perfect sense that America is leading in the willingness to ask countless questions about love. From country music to medical healing research, Americans are unafraid, cautious maybe, but basically unafraid to ask: What Is Love? and, Why Is Love?

Imagine a culture of people finally willing to go there? It was prophesized by the great paleontologist, the blessed Jesuit priest, Tielhard de Chardin, that one day when we had harnessed all other forms of energy, we would come upon the energy of love. Then, he said, we would discover fire for the second time.

We would be at the threshold of a human dimension of meaning, of living, of being, of creative cosmic identity such that we would be and are now entering the angelic realms. We are entering the realization of heaven on Earth, the spiritual purpose our species exists...and our passport, our rite, and right of passage is love.

From over here, gone yonder, none of these emergent facts for your life and times has any surprise for us. I will not say for us these truths are commonplace; I would rather say they are holyplace. But you must be feeling that the veil between you all and your sacred holiness is dawning thinner and thinner.

What an amazing moment in human evolution. Just think of the human dimensions you are becoming.

XXVII.

George Washington
1732-1799

I had bullet holes in some of my clothing but none ever touched me. I was not a great general, just a tall straight man who sat a horse as if he had been born there, a man with to me a mysterious and monumental patience. How repeated retreat can end as victory is another mystery. All I can think is that there are ways of heaven with which we are so unacquainted and ill-equipped to understand that the best we can do is try to be brave, kind and courteous while the mysteries roll forth before us.

Still, I would have to say that America is somehow a gift to humanity, despite all her cataclysmic errors and falsehoods. It is a most confusing journey she has traveled and is traveling still. If I have any personal pride, it is in the honest depth of my humility in the face of this confusion. It feels to me that when all is totally lost on the field or in the supposed halls of reason, the breath of grace reaches out and tenderly touches America so we may carry on we know not where.

It would seem, then, that the entire American experiment in self-governance rides on the glorious white steed of grace. No one knows where is the stable where that steed finds rest and reward. No one has the knowledge to call that steed forward. No one, no one rides that steed.

One might imagine, but imagine only, that there is a new political economy out ahead for America to approach formed in brave kindness and courteous generosity. One might go goodly there in prayer praying for the presence of the white steed, white as the head of the bald eagle, white as the goodness of the ocean foam.

There is in the power of Nature, a politics of the future for Americans. It is a politics inclusive of every member of the Earth's family of life. It is a politics beyond humanity of which humanity is only a humble friend. It is a politics of life salvation from which there is now no retreat.

Quiet humility, tender generosity, fierce honesty, these are the feed for the white steed of grace, these are the new virtues and values with which Americans can create a frame of friendship with all life.

This is not war, America, this is worship. The victory in worship is love.

XXVIII.

Priscilla Emerson
1926-2005

Children are grace. Feeding them is feeding grace.

Children have a grace of being, a grace of motion, a grace of laughter. The pure of heart in their innocence look out at the world with the expectation of love. Meeting that love with love is to be a parent regardless of whose child it is you are encountering. There is a great and deep joy in greeting all children with simple uncomplicated love and in feeding them when possible.

How food is prepared is another love story of great value and joy. There is also grace in the fixing and cooking of food and especially in the eating. Waking up in conscious generosity of spirit in the presence of good cooking is one of the surest ways humans will mature into their proper parenting responsibility. Response with love and joy is the only anti-depressant as powerful as just plain hard work.

A meal made and served with love is a form of love-making more important than sex. It is one of the surest ways a woman can avoid disappointment. Imagine the day when all men learn to cook for others with love and then do all the dishes and clean the kitchen. There is hope for humanity yet.

It may yet be that raising all young men to be proud cooks will be the way humanity stops killing and stops war. There is nothing effeminate about cooking. Cooking is the work of respect, affection and generosity in advance; not a bad pastime for otherwise angry thoughtless types to overcome their source of anger on purpose. Thoughtless eating is almost a sin, probably just better called stupid. Conscious eating and learning how and why everything in the family of nature eats is the beginning of a working wisdom humanity had better learn pretty soon in the creation of a kitchen of kindness for all life, or the human diet will be made to shrink to disappearance. Finding and preparing food for the full family of life is now becoming and will increasingly become the only meal humanity will serve if the God-given grace of continuing life is to be human destiny. Call it ecological wisdom, call it maturity of character, call it human fulfillment, call it starvation or call it love.

XXIX.

Robert Frost
1874-1963

Two paths diverged in a yellow wood. We chose the one less travelled by, and that has made all the difference. We will be telling years hence how that choice saved human life on Earth as a gift to us from all other life.

There are those lovely lines that stroke our souls against the fiddle of our fatality. "Along the sea sands damp and brown / the traveler hastens toward the town / and the tide rises, the tide falls." "Up on the mountain, lonesome all the time / sweet potato growin' on the honeysuckle vine." "Whose woods these are I think I know / his house is in the village though / he will not mind me stopping here / to watch his woods fill up with snow...."

There is this lovely sour sweetness to life which may yet save us. Some such taste better become at least a mild addiction, or all our subsequent suffering will to us all be senseless. Death, the ultimate drug of choice, is a best seller guaranteed, but who wants that as a daily addiction?

I, for one, like T.S. Eliot's statement that, "Poetry is an attack on the inarticulate with shabby materials." Talk about sour sweet. Poor dear words, they are truly lost children, yet together they can learn to sing and so stop their crying. Or is all singing crying? Well, some praise of God can get pretty uppidy, or is it uppity? Alleluia can sometimes fool ya.

Play, play, play, it's all in what you say. That is the tender triumphant trap of human words, of human verbs. Words are the sometimes wings of our souls. Didn't you love that sentence herein by Bucky Fuller that "love is the steel of the twenty first century"? What an epiphany.

Poetry is what gets lost in translation. Poetry is lost, words are lost, life is lost. It would seem that losing is all we can do from our very first squeak.

Wrong. Song is divinity we get to sing in harmony with that tiny think we call universe. Eight letter UNIVERSE, a little octave vast on the scale of things, what a mystery, what a gift, the sound of grace.

You would have to be pretty sour or wounded not to take some simply joy in the meaning you can make, in your love song to the cosmos.

XXX.

Hunter Ingalls
1934-2008

We used to celebrate the Feast of the Overpass up on the Interstate near our ranch in Texas. What did we know about Passover? Not much. But standing on the overpass all dressed in costumes waving at the eighteen wheelers roaring by under us, now that's America.

Trucks meet Tricks. Laughter meet Faster. Roar meet More. Poetry meet Poerty. Poerty meet Poverty. And so it goes on the great flat rolling of Texas.

I used to recite almost nonsense verse while standing on my head. What better way to get attention for a few brief moments that life is good?

The life of a poet does not get in the way of most things, it just reframes the big picture since we will all hang in there anyhow. I had some pretty serious friends who were pretty serious about some pretty serious things, but nothin' much ever got done about much ever. Seriousness is pretty good for passin' the time, but laughter beats the hell out of gloom for the sheer fun of it.

I've always thought that the purpose of love is beauty, not the other way around. Think about it. What comes after love; the new recognition of new beauty. Sure, love is wonderful, but the follow-on beauty goes on and on. A friend of mine once was looked at by a big buck deer up close with such love he can feel it still when he remembers the beauty of the scene. So, what's the boss? The love of the buck or the beauty of the buck?

I already told you I stand on my head to consider stuff. So I vote for beauty beats love. Here's why. You already are love, you don't have to do love, you already are love. Now you need something to do; so do beauty. I don't mean make beauty, although that's okay if you must, but see it on purpose.

Now I was also an art historian and teacher so I made some fuss over some of the best beauty-maker lovers. But that was just my thing, and it was too anthropocentric which is a truly bad trick we human beans play on ourselves. The bean pot of the cosmos is full of beans of which we are only one bean, which a meal does not make. Who ever heard of one bean chili?

XXXI.

Mark Twain
1835-1910

Piloting a riverboat is the great and lucky art of snag avoidance. A snag is a submerged tree that can and usually does tear the bottom out of your boat and have you all swimming in about ten seconds, which is a fine reminder to not go boating if you can't swim. Today, Americans are riding on a boat load of baloney and there's hardly one swimmer aboard. The snag is debt. The sinking is no joke. The nearest safe sandbar is upstream. Oh, pilot, my pilot, what now?

Aboard the riverboat America there is only one permanent criminal class and that is Congress. Those folks gamble more money than they have every day after stealing what they do have from you. Lately, they have begun stealing from your children and their children to come, claiming there is no such thing as debt. They have seized the pilot's wheel in the arrogant ignorance of snag denial. We are all going swimming I assure you, and many of us will drown which is no joke.

Your best bet for survival is your garden. Congress can't get your food, although they will try. A hungry Congress is surely a dangerous mob. Mob rule; what ever happened to democracy, the power of the people?

The army of the people marches on its stomach which is the same posture as an army of swimmers. America is all wet already. The empire has no clothes. We are almost all naked in the storm of stupidity that is pouring down on all humanity at large and at small wonder.

Grow your garden, jubilee all your personal debt, and build your trust in your neighbors. Stay on land. The pilots, the captains of industry are lost on the river in dumb darkness and are bound for sinking for sure. The snags of debt are too secure, all else is insecure.

Dry land is where you belong in the sun of common sense. Your garden is your only bank account in hard times ahead. Your garden is a gift to your stomach which does most of your thinking in hard times. No joke, hard times are the best times to find out who your friends are or if you even have any. Cut to the chase, life is a love story. Where have you been all these years?

XXXII.

Will Rogers
1879-1935

You know, I never met a man I didn't like. They all usually liked my ropin' tricks and I always liked them no matter. If you're just naturally foolish, it's easy to like everyone and it sure is more fun that way.

Franklin Roosevelt, you used to come hear me on stage just to hear me tease you and have a few laughs. There's two kinds of humor, one where you laugh at yourself, one where you laugh at the other fella. Of the other fella kind, there's two kinds, one mean and the other friendly. I always preferred the friendly kind. You know we're all in the same soup together.

Now, about this soup. The pots getting pretty hot pretty fast and if we're goin' to be climbin' out of the soup, we better do it pretty fast. Once she starts bubblin' and boilin', it's too late because then you are the soup and Mother Nature is the only one left at the table doing any eating.

The lariat, the ropin' rope, has its own truth and logic which has nothing to do with the political spin we're all gettin' dished these days. Political spin is a rope trick you have to watch careful or you'll be tied, all of you, both hands to a leg ready for a new branding with that famous brand: two, lazy two, P. You can't untie your hands and leg with your free leg. One free leg is damn near useless except for floppin'.

Now about this new brand on your backside. What the hell ever happened to the power of the people? Was that just a myth made up by politicians to fib you out of your natural freedom and common sense?

I don't think so. But for your sure thing, if you don't rope them first, they will rope the hell out of you.

Cowboys are just usually pretty free and savvy. But when it comes to love, they're all scaredy cats and some are right out retarded. So cowboys make lousy leaders because they can gallop away from responsibility faster and farther than any racehorse jockey I ever saw. You better find lovers for leaders or you're lost.

XXXIII.

Buddy Holly
1936-1959

Hey, hey, hey, wha da ya say? You better say somethin', you better make hay.

Oh, my little darlin's, you're in a bad way. Every day it's a gettin' closer, goin' faster than a roller coaster, love like theirs is surely gone away.

Hey, hey, hey, it's a gettin' closer, life is losin' faster than it's s'pposed to. What ya better do is sing a new song today, a hay, hay.

Every day it's a getting closer, goin' faster than a roller coaster, love like theirs is surely gone away.

Hey, hay, hay, you better start singin'with them that's a wingin', with them that's a swimmin', with that's runnin'.

You better start singing this very very day, or it ain't fair in any any way.

Every day its a gettin' closer, goin' faster than a roller coaster, love like theirs is surely gone away.

Hay, hay, hay, they're all listenin', they're all glistenin', wonderin' what your song is in the same way.

Do you have a care song, do you have a fair song, are you singin' in their very same same way?

Every day it's a gettin' closer, goin' faster than a roller coaster, love like theirs is surely gone away.

Hay, hay, hay, some day soon you'll begin to say hey, you'll begin to pray, hey.

Prayer is fair, hey, prayer is fair, hey, send your love our way.

Every day now it's a gettin' closer, goin' faster than a roller coaster, love like theirs will surely come our way.

Hay, hay, hay, we're a gettin' closer to the love we are supposed to.

Prayin' is the way, hey, Singin' is the way, hey, Lovin' is the way, hey.

Every day now it's a gettin' closer, goin' faster than a roller coaster, love like theirs will always come our way.

XXXIV.

Helene Ruthling
1903-1989

On our place in Tesuque, New Mexico called Rancho de Ni os, we raised eggs and apples and children and art. The eggs we ate. The apples mostly made cider to sell, watched over in the making by Grampa Maurer, my father. The leftover apple mash we put down in the arroyo to the delight of the bees. The children grew healthy by sleeping outdoors every night of the year in covered wagon beds out among the apple trees. The art we all made all the time for the sure delight of doing it, especially getting ready for Christmas.

Those were strange and wonderful years, especially during the Second World War, because we were Germans living simply in glorious countryside not far from Los Alamos where they were inventing the atomic bomb. We were about love at Rancho de Ni os, and the surrounding Americans knew it and never gave us much trouble during the war.

That is America at its best and big-hearted, always aware and tuned into love. Why else would we have called our place the Ranch of the Children? We took in and loved all kinds of children whose families needed our support for all kinds of reasons, some even frightening emergencies.

In the end, I cannot imagine anything more happy in my heart than loving children and watching them grow up, unless, of course, it is watching them grow up to make art. Some children grow up loving other things, but most children love to make art if given the chance and if appreciated for what they make.

You know, America is a continuous work of art, so eager and able to be beautiful and generous and worthy of repeated observation and contemplation. There is such delight in the surprise of art since art is such a glorious place to put your heart. Not so, much museum art, but heart art, the decoration of simple living. America is a vast collection of all the world's artful and inventive people, how could we possibly miss being beautiful and kind where and when you least expect it?

Art is love made visible, love made manifest. Just down the road from the making of the atomic bomb, we made our simple art and sweet cider. What a wonder is America.

XXXV.

Charles Kills Enemy
1909-1986

I was sent off the Rosebud Sioux Indian Reservation to go to boarding school where they washed our mouth out with soap if we spoke our native language. The Bureau of Indian Affairs has always thought we would be better off acting like white Americans, less trouble for them and supposedly for us.

Later I was ordained as an Episcopal minister. But I came back to Rosebud and to the Black Hills of Dakota finally to be a healer and a holy man, a medicine man, for my people. I had and have that special love of all being where it just comes natural to care for all there is, just take care of it as best a simple person can.

I had a medicine bag where I collected over the years those few things I used to pass along the holiness and health to other people and sometimes to hurting animals too. It came along that the bag itself came to have that magic that makes life whole and deep and so slow full of wonder that to touch it or carry it made one a different person in love with wonder at everything.

Of course, I took it with me to every sweat lodge I ever went to so I could give my best to the suffering souls so purified by their telling of their deepest pains of truth. When you are in a sweat lodge and it is pitch dark and the terrible heat from the hot stones brought in from the fire keeper outside the lodge makes you sweat profusely, the truth of your life comes to the surface of your being to be heard and known and acknowledged by others in the sweat. These moments are the most sacred and useful to your soul and to the wellbeing of all your people and all your relations in the family of all life.

America, her soul, is now in need of a sweat. She has so much to confess and to purify and to pray for. The deepest truth is usually the most painful in the sweating and the telling, naked to the truth.

The blood of war is a terrible truth, yet there is no resolution for the soul and for the spirit of humans in war. My given name, Charles Kills Enemy I now finally understand. The Enemy is war itself. I cry with you, I sweat with you America, that we may purify ourselves forever.

XXXVI.

Henry Z. Persons
1819-1901

I was a banker in Brattleboro, Vermont starting with a fix up there after the Depression. In all my years of banking as far as I can remember no one ever defaulted on a loan I made. But my most proud start up was the Marlboro, Vermont Music Festival. We had three musicians. Pablo Casals played the cello, Rudolph Serkin played the piano and I played the cash register.

When I died after selling my last car and eating the proceeds, I left my son a tidy bit of money on the stipulation that he spend it all in two years so that he would then have to start earning again.

People called me Zee which is what I called me too, Z. Rudyard Kipling lived nearby and people used to come to my house and ask if I was Rudyard Kipling which, of course, I was not. It got tiresome.

Still, life was good in Vermont, really good. Vermonters born or borrowed from elsewhere are a kind and tolerant lot. Tolerance is a considerable virtue by my accounting. You can get a lot accomplished among yourselves if you're tolerant of one another. Tolerance may seem a mild form of kindness but it's actually far more than that. Tolerance as a conscious approach toward neighbors and strangers is a gentle kind of encouragement. It says, go on and do what you're doing and see if it works, and if not, try again maybe another way.

Somehow I think that is pretty much why and how Vermont skipped the industrial revolution business most of the others with plenty of water and electric power got caught up in. Vermonters often just invented the tools for others to create the industrial era without building too many vast mills, some small ones, but not too many.

Tolerance may be one of the mothers of invention. Just like idealism may be one of the mothers of practicality. You have to have a well worked out dream to invest in for it to turn out a practical success. Tolerance for the continued refinement of dreams helps tool them into loving ideals like the Marlboro Music Festival. Love is the ultimate and only cash register, since love is the currency of the cosmos.

XXXVII.

Thayer Jaccaci
1893-1980

I was a swimmer and really loved it. I helped set a relay record with my team at Lawrenceville School that lasted for years. That whole-body coordination is probably what helped keep me alive as a fighter pilot in the First World War, that and a superb rear gunner in the Bristol Fighter we flew for the Royal Flying Corp in France. My brother Paul and I left the Seventh Regiment in New York City and went to join the Canadian flyers who sent us on to England. Paul and I each had seventeen victories, a record still for a pair of brothers. I never flew again after I returned home to America.

My father was an artist who also bought art work for wealthy Americans in Europe, his home. He was an art editor for both Harper's and McClure's magazines. That art interest is what inspired me to find my way into advertising where, for J. Walter Thompson Company in the Greybar Building over Grand Central Station in New York City, I handled the Eastman Kodak account for over 30 years. Over the years, we worked with wonderful photographers like Ansel Adams, Yousuf Karsh and Edward Weston.

Today I would have to say that in my lifetime I went from horse and carriage to automobile to airplane to seeing a man walk on the moon and from telegraph to telephone and television. Yet, some verities remain the same, and chief among these is love.

In the pictures we used to advertise the power of Kodak film to capture life we always showed people in such a way that their obvious love of life was radiant. Of course, we had many other triumphs, some with our high speed film when we stopped the wings of a humming bird. Once we were able to stop the wheel of a locomotive passing at eighty miles an hour but we could not use the picture because it turned out that at that spot the wheel was inches above the track; too frightening a surprise.

I think the use of visual imagery has always had love as its primal subject, even the pain and horror of war and starvation in pictures pulls from within us our instinctive caring and opening of the heart. I only hope you all will, I beg you will, learn to use your eyes to see more and more of the love that is reality.

XXXVIII.

Helen Jaccaci
1903-1982

I was a New Yorker. That's where I met Thayer, my second husband. On my side of our family we had two admirals and two bishops in the Episcopal church. One of our family ministers was Dean of the Washington Cathedral and Custodian of the Book of Common Prayer. We were in the Social Register which turned out to be useless over time, but it felt good to me for a while.

Victorian era values were a mistake, in hindsight, they left one cold and lonely. Everyone cold and lonely. Love is the only real joy in life, but hard if you are supposed to be afraid of the show of it.

Language is something that you can love and it will not disappoint you. I loved language. I loved the New York Times Crossword Puzzle. Language is where we had our best friends, a wonderful collection of English teachers from the Choate School in Connecticut. We got to know them in Madison, our country hometown on the shore of Long Island Sound, when one of them rented a summer house next door and then bought it to use for all seasons. What an eccentric group of intellectuals and word lovers those men were, what fun. One of them pretended he was his own twin brother, one named John and one named Jack. On each visit, he was the other one. He had my children believing him for years. They were also, those school masters, master tellers of ghost stories and all kinds of other hilarious jokes. They were all exceptionally popular teachers at their school and it was easy to see why.

They inspired me to do some fun inventions. Once I rented a dance hall and held a dance party where you couldn't get in if you weren't carrying an animal or a bird. Then later when we moved way on top of a hill in Vermont to a place we called Deep Freeze Farm, I organized a train ride from Rutland to our town of Wallingford for children but they had to bring a pet. Then we had a wonderful pet parade when the train stopped at our schoolyard fairgrounds.

What I loved best was to be right in the middle of a whole lot of surprises. If that isn't a pet parade, if that isn't New York, if that isn't America, I don't know what is.

XXXIX.

Margaret Holland
1938-2003

I wrote, edited and published children's books with my sister and friends.

It doesn't get any better than happy, curious children. The joy of learning to read has a whole-body excitement to it which stays with you for life. When it is brand new, it is pure ecstasy, but the passion for children's reading excitement was a lifelong ecstasy, theirs and mine.

There is really only one story, the story of all stories, the love story. But there are so many different ways to tell it with all kinds of side alleys and sometimes truly scary intrusions. Good pictures, too, make it really fun for kids when they can match the words to an image to get their visual imaginations engaged and working.

My sister and I had a method of creating new stories for books. We called it RAM: rearrange, adapt and modify. Some people got a little prickly when we did that to one of their stories, but we thought the more books, the more readers, the more readings, the more feelings of love and excitement.

My life story did not turn out all that happily, I died early of cancer. But now I know the human soul is eternal and just lives love story after love story. So my only wish is that the readers of life down there do everything everyday to bathe in the ecstasy of love. I consider America to be full of side alleys and accidents, but she is till only a love story, so I hope she reads the story of her soul out loud as always, unafraid and unashamed.

XL.

John C. Gowan
1912-1986

I was an educational psychologist. I read extensively in the accounts and descriptions of the highest states of human consciousness and revelation. I made charts and maps of the progression from the lowest states and stages to the highest. Although I never explicitly related them to the higher forms of mathematics I also studied, I did come to see a series of systemic behavior in the progressions which I once titled trance, art and creativity in one of my books.

The systemic nature of the human progression of maturation of ever more conscious spiritual awareness began to appear to me as corresponding to the general systemic nature of all the stages of increasing order experienced throughout every domain of non-human growth and development and evolution as well. Stuart Dodd, another general systems scientist, and I were going to begin collaborating on these correspondences, as he had discovered and charted an elaborate progression of increasing order in the universe. We did not live long enough to get started much beyond the beginning intuition of that increasing order.

Now we both know that all increasing order in every domain is the story of love as it progressively reveals itself evermore explicitly. That means that the consciousness or soul of a country like America, too, is on an unavoidable, irresistible path of progressive maturation which is also a progressive love story.

The idea that a self-defined and continuously creatively self-defining nation state can progress in the maturation of consciousness and love may seem improbable and even impossible. The fact is that it cannot exist even as just an idea or as an experiment without continuously maturing in love.

As another of our general systems science friends said, it is either, "Grow Or Die."

You are all now in a race for survival struggling against your own murderous toxicity and greed; yet your salvation is assured if you just awake to the love you are.

XLI.

Stuart C. Dodd
1900-1975

I was credited with being one of the founders of modern sociology, macro-sociology to be exact. I was on General Eisenhower's staff during the invasion of Italy in the Second World War. Our job was to find out who the Italians might want for their leader after the war was over. We dropped that question to the citizens on leaflets from airplanes and collected the results sometimes even before the Germans had retreated and been forced out of Italy by the Americans.

Their favorite leader was the man that brought them the evening news on the radio. He spoke beautiful Italian. Most of the Italians did not know that they were listening to English radio and the newsman was an Englishman.

Before the war, I had been a professor at the American University in Istanbul where I was able to get adherents of seventeen separate religions to worship together once a week under the simple logic and persuasion that the things that unite us are greater than the things that divide us.

After the war back at the University of Washington in Seattle, I began to go beyond sociology in my thinking and started searching for a natural leveling or step stacking of order throughout the universe. After daily calculations which now fill dozens of boxes in the library archives there in Seattle, I found a progression of numerical order from the vast expanse of atomic order all the way up to human evolution and the relative time evolved for each level. I called it in chart form The Mass Time Triangle.

Toward the end of my life, I was trying to put this exquisite increase in order I had found into musical form, but a heart attack and then my final passing which was a wonderful, exciting and calm feeling experience left that work unfinished.

If asked now to put my life and all life in creative perspective, I would say it is all love unfolding, that life is love, and all order is the progressive revelation of love revealing a sweet divinity to the universe.

XLII.

Abraham Lincoln
1809-1865

I am returned in the person of Barack Obama, and now in the person of every American alive, for you have come to the hour of your fulfillment where at long last government of the people by the people and for the people is true in the heart, soul and action of every American. You are at last awake to the cherished opportunity and responsibility to invent yourselves in justice and mercy every day, no day lost, no life lost without that fulfillment.

America now means love; it has always meant so. Therefore, justice and mercy are the bold blood of your evolving American culture, your experiment in compassion. You are now at last bringing forth on this hallowed holy land an expanding love of all life born of the blood and blessings of all who have come before you so that all who come after you shall not perish from the earth unknown.

To be known, to be known for the quality of love expressed in your daily life, that is your gift, that is America, that is your more perfect union, America.

There is no such thing anymore as race, there is only human life learning to become gift to all life. Those who cling to the concept of race cling to their own sad diminution of purpose. For yours now is to be all conductors in a symphony of planetary life wherein the sound of all other life players is your music of salvation. You cannot properly conduct the glory of all the sanctity around and within you without the ear for harmonies as old as all life on earth.

Your field to consecrate is not of battle but one of beauty. Consecrate it you must or all the ancient evolution of life which has awarded you your life will perish from the earth.

You now consecrate and usher in a new birth of freedom reaching every corner of creation. Your symphony of salvation for all life on earth has a holy ring whose bell of liberty joins all the cries of all life forms singing out their souls into the opera of eternity rising and passing not unknown, but loved.

XLIII.

Walt Whitman
1819-1892

Beauty is Salvation. Sing it loud, sing it clear.

Salvation is necessary evolution. Absent that there is darkness.

America is bloody but not dark, bloody but not dark. Moments of darkness will always pass and she will be standing tall waiting for the souls of her children to awake and to rise.

You would want a mother of invention that beautiful and that strong were you ever and always here. Salvation is the mother of spiritual expression and moral transcendence. She is waiting. She is waiting.

Come all to her shores of spirit. Rise all already here. You are all peers, so lucky the chance. She is waiting. She is waiting.

There is a world you're bound to make. There is a world brave and pure. There is a love of all things holy. All is holy, all is holy. She is waiting, ever waiting. You are holy evermore.

There is no trust in debt and money, not even fame, not even comfort, not even home and hearth can save you. Only holiness is safety, wild in mystery, pure and clear. You are holy, you are holy, ever, ever, evermore.

There is only love is holy, holy love is there of you. You will be your soul eternal free from death and free from dying, such is grace is such a mystery. Rise in love forever more.

She is waiting. She is waiting.

XLIV.

St. Francis of Assisi
1181-1226

You had heard reports of miraculous happenings in Assisi and later learned that it was the day my body was moved for reconstruction purposes in the basement of my cathedral. Some members of the World Congress of the New Age held at the Medici's Fort Belvedere in 1978 in Florence came to Assisi that day, including your oldest son, Tony, then ten years old, who all returned to Florence with the stories of miracles.

So in 1987 when you again convened a gathering you called the Florence Convocation, you came to visit Assisi yourself before your meeting which was aimed at searching for the relation between love and cosmology, the story of the forming of the universe, and between love and the emerging practice of social architecture.

Then halfway through the proceedings of the Florence Convocation, several of you came to Assisi for a day of rest and restoration. You yourself were exhausted and had a migraine headache when your cab let you out in front of the cathedral. So you went directly to the nearest small hotel in the mid-afternoon and rented a room so that you could try to sleep off your headache. After you pulled the shades in your room and put your sketch pad on the table beside the bed, you lay down and said a simple prayer to me asking for help. Four hours later when you awoke with the headache gone, you found you had written the following in your sketch pad:

> Love is infinite in experience and
> meaning.
> How could it not be;
> It is the source, substance and future of
> all being.

So if you would build anything, build it on a web of love and it will be both ephemeral and timeless, monetary and enduring.

Later on that same visit to Assisi, you also wrote in your sketch pad:

From the emptiness of the infinite came the divine order of love —Love manifest in what we may know as general principles the first of which is CONSERVATION. When God had created the architecture of Divine Order, the Great Cosmological Plan of this our universe, God gave time and place with the emergence of LIGHT. Light was then the beginning measure and substance of all things and from its perfect symmetry and harmony derived complementarity. Complementarity, Attraction-Repulsion lead to disharmony and asymmetry and the manifestation of the physical we know as our universe, held in the conservation embrace of Gravity, the first principle of Love.

Gravity is matter's memory that it once was light. Love conserves that all will return to it, to love. WILL return. WILL is the unique human earth attribute. A grand experiment in Love to see if Love is naturally Self-aware, Self-reflexive, Self-fulfilling… SELF-FULFILLING…WILL IT BE?

Then you all returned to Florence to conclude your convocation. On the final day, February 26, 1987, sitting in a large circle, you asked everyone to write then and there a brief summary statement of their ten days of learning. Before you began your own writing, you prayed briefly again to me and then you wrote:

> Love is the Breath of God, the Matrix
> of all Spirit and Matter,
> Life and Growth.
> Love is the carrier of light and all the
> divine order and purpose
> we can ever know.
> It is the symbol and the story, the letter
> and the word,
> the energy and the law, the particle and
> the wave,
> the idea and the form.
> To know it as the experience of these
> things
> and in all our human relations and
> all else we experience
> is the will of life,
> is the mysterious breath of God,
> holy, holy, holy and eternal —
> on loan to use of willful Earth.
> Will we breathe the one?

XLV.

Thomas Jefferson
1743-1826

America means love.

The word America means love.

It is time, at last, for Americans to know that meaning, and not a moment too soon.

Americans have now a reckoning with human destiny. So I will speak to you in the words of now for the terms of your destiny.

For yours are the first few generations whose guardianship of all nature is a matter of your life or death down through all eternity. You may recall that I wrote that the dead authors of any document had no earthly right to bind up the lives of the living to their conceits. Rather, every nineteen years each new generation is free and responsible to reconstitute its place in the world and of a right must do so.

Never in the course of human events has a moment occurred when America's redefinition of purpose and intent been more critical in cosmic dimensions. For you are the first humans ever to see the faint but emerging image of your own eternal extinction in the mirror of planetary nature.

Accordingly, I have come back for service to my beloved America now when you are so sorely in need of a new vision, of a new beginning. I have come back to bring you to the vision of your own natural maturation. In every human born is the potential for the parent, the mentor, the sage and the transcendent being, all stages of maturation now vital for your survival. You are learning to express those capabilities as gifts your planet must have for the improving and enduring health of the whole family of life.

I suggest that you will have to develop a totally new political economy beyond democracy and capitalism in order to save life on earth. As with the work of the founding of the blessed experiment in self-governance, America, you will all become as we were then, social architects. Your artistry will become legendary down through the ages for you will have created a planetary renaissance on purpose in less than a decade. It is my current duty to help you find the design specifications for that emerging golden age of human transformation and transcendence.

Dear ones, I would define social architecture for you as:

> Divine grace revealed in natural order used for the planning and enhancement of human fulfillment.

Divine grace, sometimes called the wisdom of the universe is, of course, love. The revelation of natural order is also always the discovery of love. I have found from those among you the scientific general systems theory of transformative growth and change throughout all of nature. This revealed natural order makes clear that the tyrannical autocracy of King George the Third and his English aristocracy had to transform into American democracy, the power of the people. In the next progressive stage, the power of "We The People" will transform in your time into the power of all life on Earth. Soon thereafter, human political economy will transform again into the power of love.

By way of a brief blessing on your coming triumphs, I offer you these following few notes toward your emerging declarations of interdependence with all life. I have echoed my original declaration of independence to illustrate how radically different your present and future times are in comparison to ours at the birth of the American nation.

A Declaration of Interdependence

When in the course of human events it becomes necessary for all people to separate from the cosmology which binds them and enter into a new cosmological understanding of the universe more primal in truth and fulfilling of their rights and needs, a common courtesy for all life requires that they state the reasons and causes that drive their separation and the discoveries that impel their maturation into new being.

We the people of Earth hold these truths to be self-evident:

All is created equal, sentient and sacred in love.

All being is endowed by its source in love with certain original rights.

Among these rights are conservation of being, creation of entropy for work, manifestation of symmetry for order, and transformation by evolution for fulfillment.

These rights and principles of cosmic origin guide the people to institute new forms of self-governance based on new political economy in resonance with and reverence for the working of love in the universe.

Governments are instituted by people for people and of people with their creative engagement for the continuous care and fulfillment of all being.

When governments fail in these sacred duties of compassion, it is the right and the necessity of the people that they change their governments to bring them forward into harmony with the honest order of love.

Book Orders

Orders for additional books may be addressed to:

Unity Scholars Media
PO Box 333
Thetford Center, Vt 05075
Email: unityscholars@securespeed.us